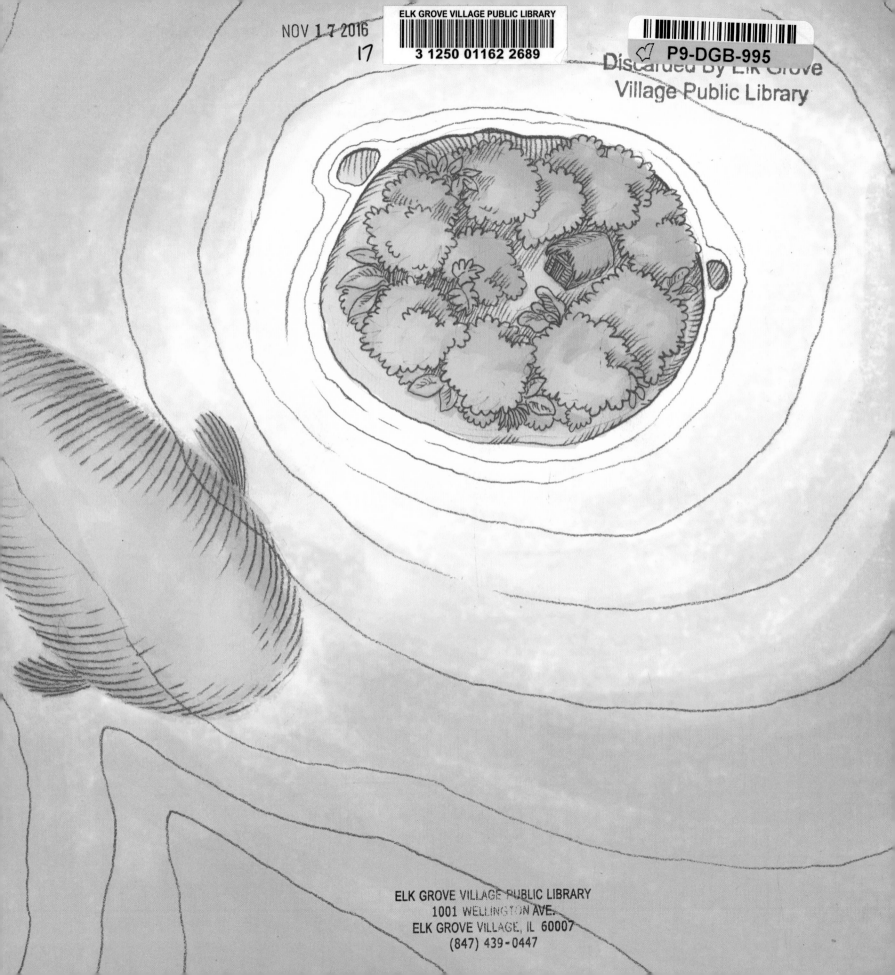

For Despina, who was on the other island

American edition published in 2016 by Andersen Press USA,
an imprint of Andersen Press Ltd.
www.andersenpressusa.com

First published in Great Britain in 2016 by Andersen Press Ltd.,
20 Vauxhall Bridge Road, London SW1V 2SA.

Distributed in the United States and Canada by
Lerner Publishing Group, Inc.
241 First Avenue North
Minneapolis, MN 55401 USA
For reading levels and more information, look up this title at www.lernerbooks.com.

Color separated in Switzerland by Photolitho AG, Zürich.
Printed and bound in China.

Library of Congress Cataloging-in-Publication Data Available.
ISBN: 978-1-5124-1793-7
eBook ISBN: 978-1-5124-1796-8
1-TL-6/1/16

dan ungureanu

Nara
and the
Island

Andersen Press USA

My home is so small, you can't lose anything.
At least, that's what my dad says.

But sometimes I felt like getting lost,

so I would go to my secret hiding place,

and look out at the other island.

Then I'd dream about how I'd get over to it.

I could make long legs and run across...

I could ask the birds to fly me there...

I could borrow Dad's bottle collection and empty the sea.

But I would have needed
a million, billion bottles.

So instead of dreaming, I always ended up feeling sad.

Or I did until today, when Dad
found my hiding place.

He says now that he's fixed our boat, we can have a real adventure.

He's going to find
the Big Fish.

It's in lots of his books, but no one has ever caught it.

And if I stay close to shore,
I can explore the island
while he rows around it.

Up close, the island is bigger...

and greener and noisier and stranger.

Full of curious shapes, funny sounds, and odd-looking things.

It's scary and I want to go home.
But then I meet the biggest surprise of all,
called Aran.

Aran says some of the funny-looking things are his best friends.

I tell him about my home, a little small and quiet, where it's hard to find a hideaway.

He tells me about his home, so noisy and wild,
that he's always trying to find a bit that's just his.

Aran has one secret place though. It's so beautiful, he's never shown it to anyone.

But maybe we could share it.

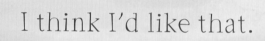
I think I'd like that.

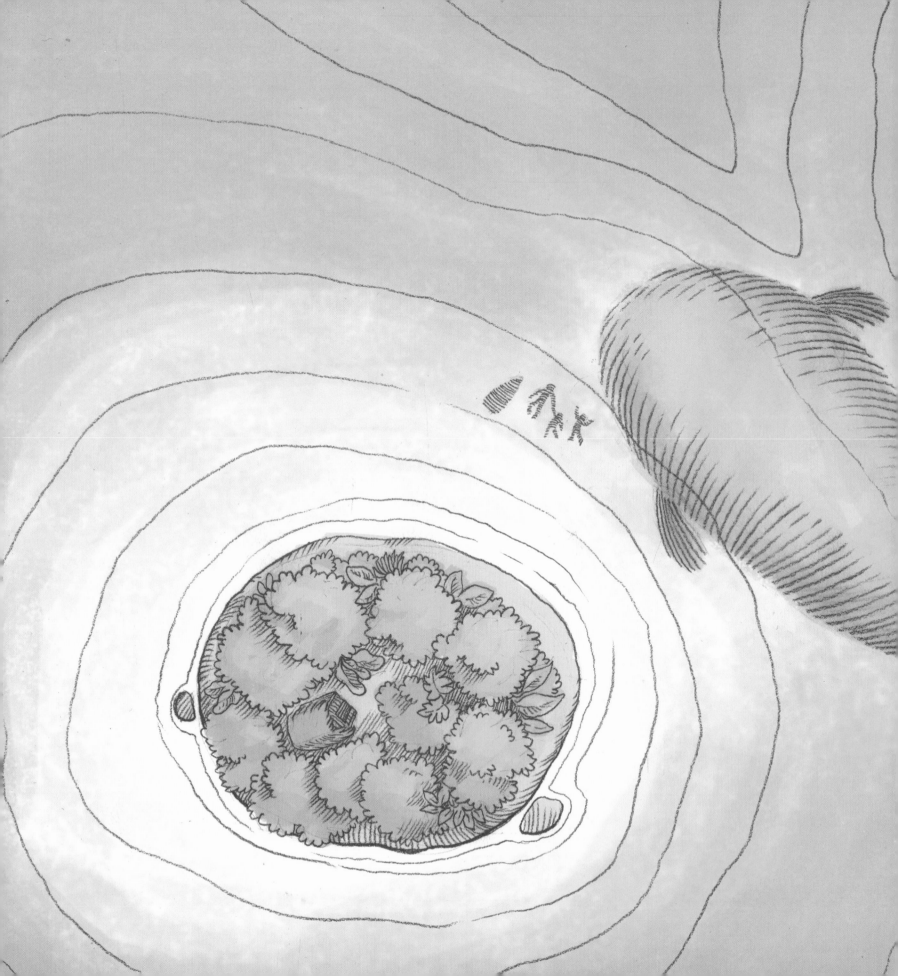